For Holly, with love ~ K W

To my beloved Grand-Maman.
Click, Clack, Croc' Geneviève! ~ J D

This 2010 edition published by Sandy Creek,
by arrangement with LITTLE TIGER PRESS

Sandy Creek, 122 Fifth Avenue, New York, NY 10011

ISBN 978-1-4351-2727-2

Printed and bound in Thailand

Lot 10 9 8 7 6 5 4 3 2 1

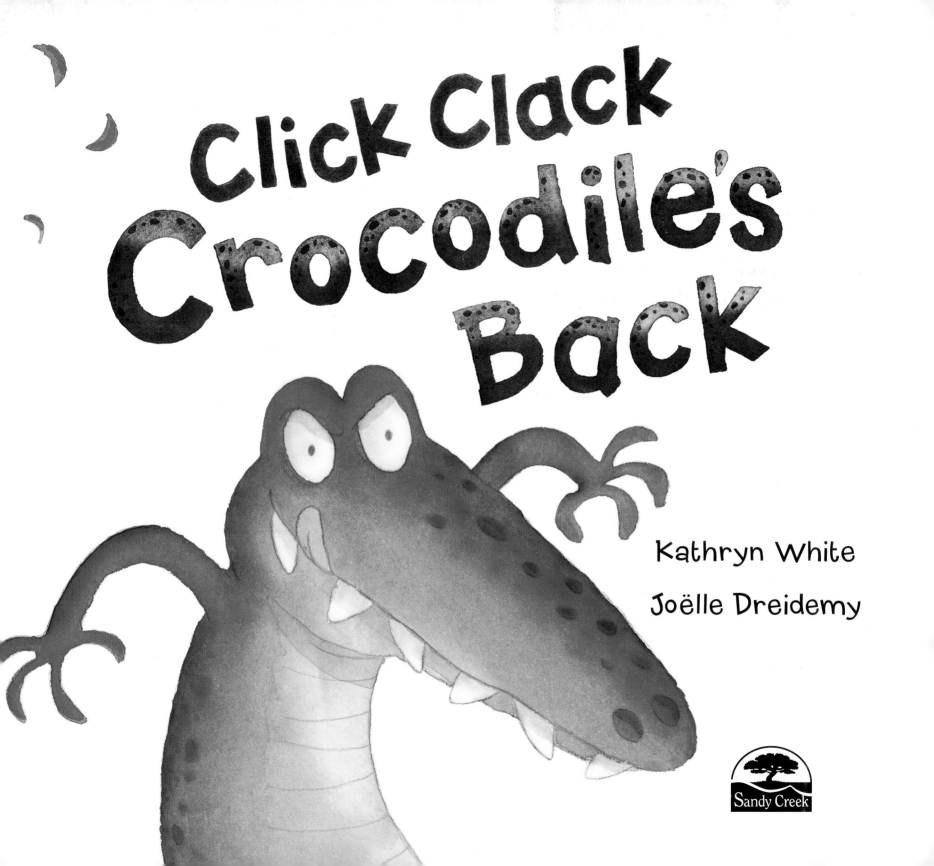

Click Clack Crocodile's Back

Kathryn White

Joëlle Dreidemy

Sandy Creek

Tremble with fear, Crocodile's near.
He's sneaking by, with a glint in his eye,
Slyly disguised as the trunk of a tree,
Ready to **snatch** you before you can **flee!**

Slip,

slap,

it's Crocodile's trap.

He's **squelching**
and **sliding**

in mud, where he's hiding . . .

Waiting to **snaffle** you
up in his claws
And **gobble** you down
with his terrible jaws!

WATCH OUT,
Crocodile's about!
Flamingos are **Preening**
then one of them spies,

Down in the rushes,
two **mean,**
greedy eyes . . .

"He keeps **creeping** up on me," Elephant groans. "That **big, sneaky** Crocodile," everyone moans.

But Monkey is cool,
Monkey is clever –
He has a plan they can
all do together.

So brave little Monkey
swings down to the river.

"A gift for Crocodile,"
he says with a shiver.

"A **gift**?" says Crocodile,
very unsure.
"Why . . . I've never been
given a **gift** before."

Monkey holds out his **trembling** hand.
"This present will make you look
wonderfully grand.
It's a jacket I made from banana peel."

Crocodile grins
and says,
"Simply ideal!"

"We've made you a hat!" the flamingos flock in,
Making a **mess** and a terrible **din**.

And Crocodile roars,
"Oh, won't I look great?
I'll be **dashing** and **sporty**
and so **up-to-date!**"

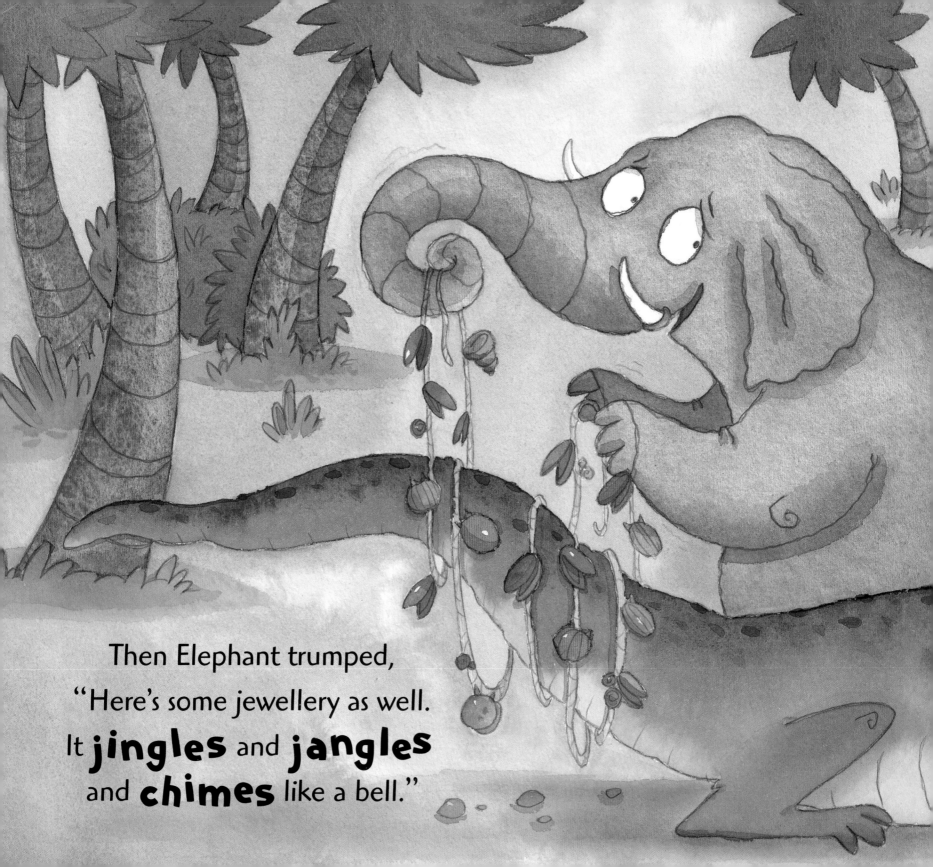

Then Elephant trumped,
"Here's some jewellery as well.
It **jingles** and **jangles**
and **chimes** like a bell."

"OH WOW,"
says Crocodile
with a big smile.
"Now I'll go **hunting**
in **fabulous** style!"

"And won't you look **fabulous**," everyone cheers,

"When you wear these new coconut charms on your ears?"

"Awesome!" says Crocodile,
giving a

grrrowl,

"I'll wear them each time
I go out on the **prowl.**"

So Crocodile grinned
and his **greedy** eyes shone,
As he shot off to try
all his new presents on.

Shhhhh!

Listen – what's
making that sound?

It's **jingling**
and **jangling** and
prowling around.

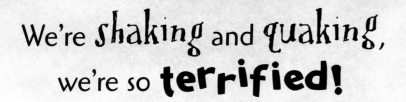

We're **shaking** and **quaking**,
we're so **terrified!**

It's a wild, crazy animal.
RUN FOR IT! HIDE!

Click, clack, Crocodile's back!

In his necklace and jacket, and earrings and hat.

He can't catch his dinner — he's tried and he's tried . . .

But everyone's heard him and run off to **hide!**